John Byrne Leicester Warren

Eclogues and monodramas; or, A collection of verses

John Byrne Leicester Warren

Eclogues and monodramas; or, A collection of verses

ISBN/EAN: 9783337304423

Printed in Europe, USA, Canada, Australia, Japan

Cover: Foto ©Andreas Hilbeck / pixelio.de

More available books at **www.hansebooks.com**

ECLOGUES

AND

MONODRAMAS.

OR,

A COLLECTION OF VERSES.

By WILLIAM LANCASTER.

London and Cambridge

MACMILLAN AND CO

1864

PREFATORY NOTE.

THE writer neither claims for nor prefixes to these verses the ambitious title of poems. They are merely rythmical exercises which have amused his leisure hours. Such an explanation is necessary by an entire misconception of a previous volume of his by a writer in the *Saturday Review*,* who chose there to designate this as 'a collection of great pretension.'

This is the only piece of adverse criticism from which, with all confidence, the writer claims exemption for this and for his previous volume.

The title of the present collection was suggested by the table of contents to Southey's collected works.

· Nov. 1 8

CONTENTS.

	PAGE
The King's Monologue	1
The Nymph's Protest	7
Country Philosophy	12
A Lament for Adonis	20
The Nameless Picture	25
Anchises	32
The Mother's Advice	38
Ariadne	43
The New Ahasuerus	49
The Apotheosis of a Town Hero	53
Rosamond	57
Dædalus	69
The Lament of Phaethon's Sisters	74

CONTENTS.

	PAGE
James and Mary	77
Niobe .	96
The Sale at the Farm	101
The Strange Parable	111
The Naiad	117
Daniel before Belshazzar	121

THE KING'S MONOLOGUE.

HEAR this, ye idle nations, and be still;
    Hear this, unstable children of revolt;
My voice is with you yet a little time.
I have worn out the marrow of my days
Unrecompensed, unreverenced; evermore
I am a broken life and dispossessed
Of filial adoration in my wane.
Ye run to any light and hail it guide,
Ye march for any ensign under heaven,
And learn rebellion with a bestial zeal;
Prone in contagion to a blinder doom

B

Ye perish from the precincts of the land.
Therefore have I been patient from disdain,
And slow to chide with weakness; I have made
Revenge forgiveness, when some wounded thing
Lay in the shadow of my sword to die.

Still I forgave and still ye vexed my soul
With wayward fluctuation, anarchies,
And panic tumults in the dead-ripe noon
Of cloudless safety. Ye are wholly seed
And stock of discord: I am weary now.
Leave me a little rest before I sleep.
Effort is food and honey to the young:
They breathe by action; but the old man folds
His mantle, storing breath in utter peace.

Consider, Heaven, that these have set my days
A discord, this my state a bitter thing,
And made my spirit hungry for repose.
Can they remake my cunning hours again,

Or build me ramparts from the dark event?
Pale is my sun: I care not to endure.

Is it a little thing that ye are sway'd
By me who spake with minds of larger mould,
Sons of the silent years whose race is low,
Inheriting their wisdom to command?
Hereafter ye shall love me in the dust,
A late obedience, and desire my voice.
Then shall one speak above my crownless head,
'He hath ungirdled to his last repose
The sword of empire, but our after kings
Have shrunk to draw the blade and there it rusts.
And he was wise as the strong wise of eld,
No puny cackler: surely he had changed
The voice of council with the ancient wise,
And grew as these to council, who no more
Resume their strength and everlasting name.'
Thus in late years perchance effectual praise
Shall reach my mansion with the frequent dead

I have accomplish'd empire to the verge
Of mortal change, and consecrate to peace
The moments of irresolute decay.
I fail the childless father of my realm :
My memory is my sole posterity,
My deed the stable land-mark of my name,
My work, my heir; so best, than if my race
In everlasting generation ruled
Unchallenged treasure thro' the forward years,
As gods, in firm abiding, dignified
With kingly works the children of their thought.

The old man withers : ye forget his power.
Have I not chain'd my rivals round my state,
And made the kings of nations, more than these,
Famish in burning purple for revenge ?
Have I not laid an ordinance of doom
On all resistance, task'd my foes as slaves,
And link'd their functions to a thorny curse
Of sleepless renovation ? Has this arm

Shrunk to extirpate in a mean remorse
The seed of alien armies, merciful
To my rebellious children's realm alone !
I led your hosts and I have spoken fire
To congregated phalanx, on the edge
Of conflict, swaying like wind-furrowed reeds:
My glance was as the lifting beam of day,
Numbering the faces in their van to die.

I am old now, dismantled and declined,
And stripling feet are itching to ascend
The steps of this imperial canopy.
Shall I speak false and smoothly at the last,
Cease with a recent lie between my teeth,
Die with a smiling falsehood on my face ?
Shall I unspeak my nature for an hour ?
Such as I am ye know me and have known.
Age is untutor'd to repeal defect,
And alteration pain in ancient eyes,
Pain to dethrone old purpose at the last,

Pain to untread the ordinance of years.

Be more obedient and forgive my scorn:

Somewhat I love this people that I scorn.

Behold I guess not to whose hand ye fall;

Obey him, prosper, leave my bones in rest.

THE NYMPH'S PROTEST.

WHY art thou fallen, sacred earthborn might,
    Craft of the noblest, wherefore hast thou failed ?
The earth-born Titans fell, and nature's voice
Moaned in the new supremacy of Zeus.
But a disdainful Atè-vengeance came,
And floated like a dream about his halls
On to the amber tables and the rest
Of that Elysian feasting : but they sat
And shuddered by their wine with joyless eyes,
Above the cloud-rack in the belted rose
And orange vapours, loathing food divine.

But she, the curse of Atè, came not on
'Mid those soft-bosomed meadows where the race
Of heroes, in conclusion grandly calm,
Eternally repose.

               Deck out thy heavens
With rainbow gleams, thou tyrant: build thy rest
Securely: bid the scented asphodel
Feign a wan summer where no winter enters.
Thou canst not be the tyrant of that fear,
Coeval with thy reigning, which shall plant
Thy feet on thorns amid the heavenly flowers.

For us no hectic summer of the gods,
But real earth, imperfect, bountiful,
Its deaths and its renewals; let us breathe
Apart, long sundered from the haughty seat
Of thy predominance and withering power,
God-queller Zeus, whose mercy is a dream.
Give us the kindly earth, its fleeting love,
Love tho' a mortal one; and hand in hand

Tread we the pleasant pastures, and out-tell

With tender vows the number of the stars.

Or bind, all breath and soul, eternal oaths,

That may not last the changes of a moon;

And our hot kisses and the clasping hands

Shall be as revelations on the soul

Of something that perfection cannot give,

Earth-savouring, earth-imperfect, yet to us

Worth all the sameness of a stale Olympus.

Love is alone eternal as the stars:

The tyrant cannot touch it: to its age

His puny throne is builded but an hour,

His generation is a recent thing,

His dynasty a growth of yesterday.

My mortal lover, look into mine eyes,

Look deep into mine eyes, wert thou a god,

I could not love thee more, I ask no more:

Be with me always, always, 'tis enough.

Leave me this earth, this love, and rule thou on
The weary clouds, unenvied and supreme.
Crush down the gentler race of nature's gods
In everlasting darkness, whose sole crime
Was to have ruled ere thou didst rule. Their name
And very record galls thee on thy throne
With silent protest at the upstart king.
Their patient foreheads seam'd with scoring flame
Sustain'd benignant empire ere thy day:
And this men know and teach their sons to teach
Their children, how the order of this world
Harmonious once, lies groaning in thy sway;
How, hating this remembrance, thou hast bound
The elder powers in darkness, vainly wise:
Torture thou canst but not abolish these.

But me the patient earth, that bears thy hand
And stormy desolation, shall console.
The woods shake off their thunder-rain and stand
In their divineness: thee the sacred sun

Owes nothing for the radiance round his head;
Thou canst not tear him from the arch of heaven
And make the nations darkness. Spring is here
Without thee, and the myriad blossoms spread
As if thine evil were a thing unknown.

COUNTRY PHILOSOPHY.

WILLIAM AND JAMES.

WILLIAM.

GOOD morrow, neighbour, 'tis a tuneful morning:
  The birds have jump'd into their singing gear
Most suddenly, and spring, before our thought,
Comes with the wheatear on the fallow side.

JAMES.

I told my wife that I should find you here
On the first blackbird's whistle, and I came

And here I find you: let us chat an hour:

This is no busy season to our hands—

Time to look round, and little else to do

But breathe sound air and broaden like green corn.

What power this March sun shakes upon our path.

WILLIAM.

Lean on this boundary hedgerow of our farms.

We are near enough for talking: I can watch

My beasts at graze, and you can count your stacks,

Your feet upon your holding, mine on mine.

JAMES.

William, I think I've slipped a score of years

Since yesternight: this touch of frost has given

A spice and savour to the calm serene,

And makes the sunshine burnish on the hedge,

Or 'tis my fancy. I'm as fanciful

This morning as a youngster of eighteen—

There goes one: listen, down the lane, to the right

He whistles, now he sings by breaks, "Fair lips
Whom are ye for, if ye are not for me?"

WILLIAM.

This hawthorn bird is out before the buds
That feed him; for the thorny twigs are bare
That nurture up their blossoms near the tread
Of feet that pause not earthwards for delight,
When blooms of may shower on the clasping hands,
Or blind those eyes from forward-searching care.

JAMES.

Why, friend, you have that from some book of songs.

WILLIAM.

Not I; the air's to blame; if some old thrush
In spring forgets his hoarseness into song.
I shall be mute enough by harvest week,
With other occupation than at ease
To lounge and pipe a careless flourish here.

JAMES.

Each month has office in the farmer's year,

And chief in this I count our calling best,

That nature's scope and change are all our own,

And so we cannot lack variety.

See yonder townsman in his warehouse walls:

What change, except in his thermometer,

With wet or burning pavement, marks his days

Or notes the deeper year; and gives him rest

From that eternal simper at his wares

When customers bite briskly?   He shall see,

From zero to the dog-day weather-point,

One patch of sky.

WILLIAM.

And yet this very man

Secure in his importance, holds us cheap

As bumpkins, speaking broad, with swollen hands,

And counts his apeish mincings as the trick

Of true gentility, 'what clowns are these.'

JAMES.

I would not wear his manners for a week

To be a squire a twelvemonth and a day;

Content to be no better than my father,

And, thank these hands, no worse, to pay my way

And move about my pastures in no fear

Of bailiffs or the rent-day, with a son

To take the old place on when I am gone,

And keep a stranger from the fields where I

Have been a boy and grew a man and died.

WILLIAM.

Your scheme of life is brother to my own;

I shall not change my trade, tho' it has rubs

And stiff ones: now this agent of our squire's,—

The man was born to plague me, and his thought

Comes like a city whiff to taint in smoke

The freshness of the morning,—well this man,

Whose soul is in his pockets, and whose eyes

Purblind to aught but stiff arithmetic,

Would have me square my hedgerows like a rule,

And prune to faultless parallelogram

The wilderness of May-bloom and its nests.

'Cut straight that curving brook,' quoth he, 'it wastes

A good half acre; clear the rubbish growth

That cumbers round its reaches; let it run

In ship-shape current like the squire's main-drain:'

I cannot keep my temper with the man:

We'll change the subject.

JAMES.

       O, I let him talk

Above his gases and his phosphate base,

His lime and silicon: it pleases him

And prints well in the 'Herald' with this head,

'The chemistry of farming:' yet this man

Of mighty theory is but a babe

In practice; I have seen him over-reach'd

By very shallow knaves: this wordy man

Bought at the fair last week a flock of ewes

Not worth a halter.

WILLIAM.

Serve him richly right :
And yet the squire shall keep him after this;
He'll talk him round in his smooth fluent way:
Well it's no gear of mine.

JAMES.

The world flows on,
And in its stream some dregs waft uppermost.
But truce to these discomfortable themes :
Look round, forget them : timid spires of green
Creep thro' the fallowy ridges, frail to bear
One dew-drop's burthen, yet shall these prevail
Weak infants of the harvest to the full
And stately ear, to clothe the upland side
As with a forest-sea, wherein the breeze
Has visible workings, and the cloud is seen
To mask and free the light in gleamy falls.

WILLIAM.

The morning draws, and we have paid enough

In leisure to its freshness.   I must set

Some graftings in my orchard, whence my son,

Who knows? shall reap the apples—now—farewell.

But as I go one word—that boy of yours

Is very often at our place of late :

I may not think his early schoolfellow

My son his main attraction ; and our Jane

Is smartened up I fancy when he comes.

Well, well, let things fare on : but well I know

If there is aught in this I shall be glad,

And you I think, James, will not take it ill.

A LAMENT FOR ADONIS.

WE will lament the beautiful Adonis;
　　The sleepy clouds are lull'd in all their trails.
The brooks withhold their violet glassiness.
The branchy volumes of the clouded pines,
Like drooping banners, in excess of noon
Languish beneath the forehead of the sun :
Nor dares one gale to breathe, one ivy-leaf
To flicker on its strings about the boles.

　　Lament Adonis here in dead-ripe noon ;
Weep for her weeping, Queen of love and dream,
Disconsolate, love's ruler love-bereaved :

Where is thy godhead fallen, what avail
To throne it on the clouds yet lose thy joy?
Couldst thou not hold Adonis on thy lips
Eternally, and scorn the ebbing years!
This, this were meed of immortality,
To wear thy stately love secure and fair
Of rainy eyes: now shalt thou ne'er resume,
Enamoured Queen, thy shelter at his heart:
His arms no longer Aphroditè's nest.

Kneel then, and weep with her and weep with her.
It is not meet that pure cheek's crimsoning,
It is not fate those bloom-ripe limbs endure
The stain of thick corruption and the rule
Of common natures: Queen, possess thy power,
Raise him beyond the region of the sun;
There cherish back the heavy eyes to blend
With that full morning of the ageless gods:
Watch him to life in bloomy asphodel,
Dissolve thy soul on his reviving lips.

In vain, 'tis idle dreaming this shall be.
In vain, ye maidens, this our sister toil
To scatter posies on his sacred sleep
With dole for him that was so beautiful :
He shall not wake from that lethean dream :
He shall not move for her immortal smile,
Nor hear the busy kisses at his cheek :
She ceases and she sobs upon her hands :
Come, let us weep with her and weep with her.

Smother his head with roses as he lies.
The day may draw the sacred twilight down :
The dew-lights on the grasses and the leaves
May speck the woods, as night the sky, with stars ;
The sun-down gale shall not, because we weep,
Forego his perfume, or night's bird her song.
Nature is greater than the grief of gods,
And Pan prevails while dynasties in heaven
Rule out their little eons and resign
The thunder and the throne to younger hands.
He is the rock, but these the rounding waves.

Lament not, Queen of love, lament no more :
Nature and love alone are ageless powers ;
Thy queendom, Aphroditè, shall not fail.
The reign of might shall fail, the wisdom fail
That wrought out heavenly thrones : the weary clouds
Shall not sustain them longer : only love
And nature are immortal.   Nature sealed
Adonis' eyes : the kindly hand forgave
The creeping years that held Tithonus old
Before the smiles that loved him.   We revolt,
And chide at wisdom in our shallow tears :
Content thee : surely better so to cease,
The riper years enjoy'd, the refuse left,
Secure of stain and blemish and decline.
Have comfort, Queen, though love will not endure
To lighten loss in reasoning out despair.

Have comfort ; and our homeward choir shall hymn
Thy godhead thro' the cedarn labyrinths
Till they emerge upon the flushing sheet

Of sunset : on those waters many an isle

And cape and sacred mountain, ripe with eve,

Cherish thy myrtle in delicious groves :

Infinite worship at this hour is thine.

They name thee, Aphroditè, and the name

Blends with the incense towards the crimson cloud.

THE NAMELESS PICTURE.

'YOU say this picture never had a name!
 I like it best in all the gallery:
More than the faces of Italian saints,
More than the genial Flemings by their fire,
Its plaintive and most touching pensiveness
Prevails upon my fancy: this must mean
A portrait surely: the reality
Of desolation in those girlish eyes
Is no ideal study. Can it be
A family picture? you reply, that these
Are hung together in the entrance hall

The style and dress would give some thirty years
Since this was painted. Why, you told me now
That you had been a servant in this house
More time than that : come, you know more of this :
I am a stranger here, and from to-day
Return no more : this confidence is safe
With one who cannot break it : tell me all.'

Then the old servant faltered and refused ;
But more the stranger pressed him, and at last •
He spake to this effect :

'Some thirty years, ay, more than thirty years,
That painting I remember : then it hung
In my young master's room where first he saw
It waking : and whole days when he was sad,
And that, poor boy, was often, or the squire
Had vexed his son with crotchets and ill pride—
Then, days and days, a silken veil concealed
The painted features : now the veil is gone.'

'And I remember how a rumour grew

That Robert, the old man had plann'd it long,

Should wed a neighbour heiress, and she came

To visit with her people in full trim,

And we supposed the thing as good as done.

But Robert on the morning that they left

Went to his father's study: in an hour

He came upon me with a stormy face,

And bade me pack for London on that night;

But the old squire left not his room again

Till we were gone: I never saw him more.

'We had not been in town above a week—

It might be more: I think it was a week—

I was alone with Robert in the house,

His only servant, and the house was small;

When at the edge of dusk a lady came

And wished to see my master: at her face

I started as at some unearthly thing,

The face had left its canvas at the hall.

'When she had talked with Robert for a time
He led her down to go; and as they past
My room she seem'd to pause, and then these words—
I could not choose but listen, for the voice
Drave some strange power upon me, and the sounds
Seemed one by one to burn into my brain
And could not be forgotten. Thus she spoke:

'"True friend, forget me: I am not mine own:
Seek out some worthier one and leave this dream:
Forget the gentle time that we have known.
You know I have forgiven long ago:
Nay, what should I forgive? You made me love
And have been very true: shall love and truth
Demand forgiveness? What had been my life
Without thee and before thee? O mine own,
My one true love, shall I complain of thee
Noble and young, to whom my passionate heart
Fled tremulously happy; over-blest
That thou wouldst smile upon so mean a thing,

Unworthy thee save in her utter love!

I have dared to see thee once, I have dared to speak,

And tell thee that this marriage shall not cease

For one like me.   I will not drag thee down,

I love thee far too much to drag thee down,

Or hold thee from thy station to resume

The pleasant hours beside me: not for me

Thy people shall reproach thee: truest friend,

I know thy utter fealty to refuse

The sacrifice, if any choice were thine,

So I have left thee none: the die is cast.

He is a worthy man my husband—I

Am better so, than plaguing thee, a clog

About the neck I love, too lowly born

To wed with thee, and yet too fondly proud

To bar thee from advancement and thy right.

Fear not for me, if I can say farewell,

Truest and best and dearest, long farewell."

'Then silence; and I heard her lessening feet

The door was closed, and then, methought, there came

A sound of heavy falling, and I went

And found my master senseless on the stone.

Poor lad, he never rallied from that day,

Altho' he seemed to all the world but me

The same as ever, only somewhat still,

And paler than his wont. From day to day

He fought his sorrow down, but still it grew

And mastered : in his absent way he said

Half to himself one night, and half to me :

" I wish I had the heart to face again

My father : they have written, the old man

Is very feeble lately : he and I

Are lonely in the world, and shame it is

To bicker with each other, for of friends

We have not many else." And that day week

A letter came to tell the squire was dead.

' Then we returned to this old place with speed.

And the old squire was buried, with a score

Of coaches, lines of tenants, in the pomp
Of a great landlord.   Robert lived alone
Thereafter many years—that room was his.
Poor lad, I wondered that he lived so long.
He ever seemed to carry where he went
A weight of evil : and a vague suspense
Held in his eyes, as if he waited long
For something that should come but never came :
And yet a gentler master with it all
I think we shall not find—But I am long :
He died a young man still, and then the place
Past to a distant cousin.   The old breed
Is gone and ended out, and these I serve
Are strangers : not unkind, for me they kept,
I had been here so long and here would die.
And now you know the little I can tell
About the portrait.'

ANCHISES.

LEAVE me, my son, an hour in loneliness
    On this Sicilian Eryx: my farewell
Of earth is near accomplished: I would hold
Communion with the faces of the past,
Collect my soul in memory ere I go,
And feed on shadows of the ancient years.
Here underprop thy mantle to my head,
For here the mountains have a lonely sound,
And like faint harmony the wash of sea:
Return thee in an hour, return my son.

    I die in a strange land: a casual grave

Where never son of mine shall talk or tread

Hereafter, and no kindred step impress

My lonely bones. I have left my fathers' urns

As far behind me as the rising sun,

To measure distance by the painful sense

Of travel to the pausing limbs of age.

I do remember when my country fell,

They snatch'd me thro' the tumult to the ships.

Æneas strode before them, many a Greek

That barr'd his passage died : but my old blood

Glow'd not to see them fall, as in the days

When battle lit my soul like maiden's lips.

Mine eyes were dim, I only could complain

At fair endeavour wasted to ensure

A wither'd abject from the sword to-day

Whose urn is due to-morrow, and I said :

"All is disorder'd like an ancient tale,

And the old form of time is cracked and thrown

Dishonoured by. Confusion big with death

Usurps our hearths, and draws a line of blood

Across the record of our dearest hours.

There is no further sorrow to endure,

No tear beyond what I have seen to-day:

Thrust me in mercy thro' and let me rest

In Trojan earth: most old am I to change

My country: ye are young, your years are sweet,

But mine are very weary: what reward

Of voyage mine except a stranger grave?

A scratch will end me: 'tis an easy boon.

Is it no bitter thing, this ancient frame

Condemned upon the threshold of its dust,

To ride the wild heads of the hollowed waves,

The lapse and weather of the scaling seas?

When all discomfort multiplies on ache

Of waning years, stiff burden in themselves."

But they or heard me not or would not heed.

Thence, in the curving buffet of the tide,

Our keels have girdled half the seas in quest

Of visionary kingdoms, with reward

Of infinite misfortune to our hands.

We set the sail for other thrones, beyond

The sea-mark of the rolling spheres in heaven,

And found no scant of danger or of death;

But reap this sole unenvied royalty,

To be the chief of mortals that endure.

O stedfast son of thine unstable sire,

Dost thou misdoubt the shielding God's command,

That led thee out among tumultuous seas,

Still pointing onwards? Oracle of heaven,

Care dost thou build us, in each port new care:

Where is that utmost haven of thy word?

Peace, be content, old heart, what shouldst thou do

With future? Cheat no longer closing eyes

With lust to see the kingdom of thy son.

In the next valley or beyond the stars

'Tis one to me: my wounded life admits
No interim to reach it: here I pause.

   No farther: be it then: my way is done.
Turn, ancient eyes, turn backwards ere your sleep;
I, the old man, would number back the years
Of all my flower and strength and nervy prime,
Heroic—once heroic and thus now.
Erase, old heart, the staining years between,
Face thy great hours once more, then cease to beat:
Nay, rather let large silence hold the past:
Its changeless veil removes not for the moan
Of retrospect, and weak it were to fear
Immutable conclusion wholly best.
Behold my son returns, and I will smooth
These doubtings from my face: enough for me
The question and the anguish: this were shame,
To dash his living purpose with the taint
Of this my palsied fancy and mistrust—
Courage, my son, to-morrow we will spread

New sails, the land of promise sure is near.

If my breath hold till sunrise I will sail

Not less than the young soldier in the fleet:

If I have slept by then, large choice of grave

Is here upon the beach; but sail not less,

My spirit leading to the fated land.

THE MOTHER'S ADVICE.

I HAVE heard you out, my boy; now let me speak.

    We are alone together, you and I :

So we have been : the new tie changes all.

You are not pledged as yet ? So far is well—

Nay now, be patient, hear me till the end :

I do not mean to gainsay with one word

Your marriage as a marriage : 'tis the way

And process of the world : the mother's turn

Cedes to this stronger heritage of time,

And the wise mother grieves not : only this,

I deem it in my duty chiefly now

To mind you how past things have stood with us,

To argue out your future as I may
In all forbearance where I see you touch'd
So nearly: therefore hear, my boy, and weigh
The words as calmly as the words are said.
It is my right and duty to advise
Tho' hardly to forbid: these few calm words
And I have done: yours is it to decide,
The sequel good or evil most is yours:
And as you say hereafter so shall I.

For when your father died, and left the land
Encumber'd, you had been at school a year,
And you and I were lonely in the world
And very poor at first: the place is small,
The income scarce enough to hold our heads
Above the yeoman, but the name is old,
And you at least are born a gentleman;
But one so little rich this name can bring
No license to be idle. This alone
Were profit more than loss, if this were all.

Weigh then, my son, her station with your own,

To her in fairness weigh it while you may.

Most free am I of narrow county pride,

That mates by pedigree, and would despise

Earth's fairest choice with no armorial stem;

But this at least allow me to premise,

As something in the scale of yes or no,

Her grade is not as yours: tho' young and fair,

The daughter of a village lawyer, still

She is not much to bring me for your wife

Without a dower to this bare manor-house,

Whose crumbling rafters chide their needy lord.

You answer this is worldly: love is more

Than birth the mock of accident: that she

In the sweet garland of her youth outpays

A labyrinth of lineage, and the dross

Of mercenary heirdom: this is well,

And gallant speech, and easy to uphold

While yet her flower has freshness: pause on this,

And look beyond: for what is man removed
Above the herd, who fears to reason out
The franchise of his foresight? Think on this,
Will her disparity be held as light,
As now you hold it, in the testing days
When she has lost her beauty? Dare romance
Make equal all in love and turn foresworn
After a few rough years? No better then
Than he who never made pretence to love
And wedded for advantage.

                    O my son,
Think me not hard and worldly: I have known
That poverty beyond the poor man's curse,
Which makes the needy gentleman forego
His rest to save appearance with the world,
Nor shame at last an honourable name.
And strong must be that wedded love to save
Its gloss in such misfortune: such was ours,
Your father's, portion: yours, alas, my son,
Not greatly fairer; therefore, bear with me,

If, having known the bitterness, I teach
The peril to my child. I am not hard
Tho' I have had my troubles: I can feel
For your young love and you, altho' my voice
Must sound from duty with a raven croak
Among your may-bloom weather. I have said:
Decide my son, in wisdom, I have done.

ARIADNE.

LO, at my feet this ocean, and the moon
   Is shaking out her splendours on its fields.
The spring is sighing up beneath the earth,
And settles in the winter of my soul
With tumult and with impulse, but no joy.
The mountain streams are reeling to the sea,
They make a voice on night beyond the wind.
I question with the wilderness of stars
For comfort. These eternal pinnacles
That toss the striding Neptune from their walls
Have heard the protest of my lonely tears.
There is a cliff that wrestles like a god

Alone in waters, for the waves have rent

His brothers down behind him, and alone

Cinctured with mutinous discord evermore

He feels the teeth of everlasting surge

Eat out by inch his earth-roots till he fall.

Even such a weary purpose is my life,

Opposing isolation, tho' it knows

An hourly gaining sentence at its core.

Is there no rest? surely in craggy bowers

Apart from moonlight rest the dissonant waves:

The sea-mew builds in rifted silence there,

And makes her brood a safety: whom her mate

Will not relinquish though the open seas

Invite the sinew of his reaching wing.

Patience is half ignoble in much wrong.

These gods, that vex our wretchedness, exact

This further torment, that the victim's lip

Tell not its pain but bless them for their curse.

These, while the surfeit of prosperity
Crowds all their altar-steps with hecatombs,
Forbid the wretched franchise to complain.

This man—this hero—for he wore the name
Gilded with deeds in Crete, and lack'd the heart
Heroic, masking guilt in smoothest show—
This eminent concealment of dishonour,
Theseus, the name will burn my uttering lips,
I brand thee rich in worship as a slave
Whose hands are full of lies and infamy.
Be demigod in shallow Hellas still:
'Tis the world's process to make great men small
And worship draff, and kneel to ready knaves
Who steal an empty throne, and seated cry,
"I am a god, come, worship!" and men come.

So rule in Athens, Theseus, and the herd
Shall burn their abject incense to thy state.
Be lawgiver of nations: blazon out

Thy virtue : state has seasons of repose
And breathing for the actor, intervals
Secure of note, to revel out the wrong
Most native to thy nature and resume
The Theseus I have known thee, brave alone
In cheating foolish maidens from their homes,
And leaving death most ready to their hands
When thou art weary, hero, and away.

So let me live though weary of myself,
To thee at least dishonour. Silent years
May dim my features on thy memory :
But not that long eternity of time
Can sweeten thought and record of my wrong,
Enduring in the pauses of thy brain
When idler themes are absent. I have said :
And through the shout of thy triumphant hour
A whisper of my name shall tear thee down,
And teach thee what thou art, though men acclaim
Thy glories to the citadel of God.

Enough of thee: be faithful to thyself:

Poison more lives and banish all thy rest.

But I perforce live on, perforce consume

The barren gift of breath, and watch the years

To winter; whom the folding of a flower,

The burning dew-drop, sudden daffodil,

The golden weather dropt among the woods,

Affect with no delight: all pleasant things

Are equal apathies.

               O rest and peace,

Fabled beyond the sunset, equal gods,

Dare I entreat you thus with sleepless eyes

And such a seething heart? Ye will not come:

The perfume of immortal asphodel

Pervades your meadows, and ye will not come.

To me the moaning seas and barren strand

Must minister their comfort, and the sounds

Of nature recompense the absent voice

Of human consolation. I have seen

The slow wave wear the rugged cliff to smooth,

The weak rain batter out eternal stone :

Where nought endures shall only sorrow build

An ageless throne above the fallen years?

THE NEW AHASUERUS.

WHERE is the rest and whither all this tending?
    To be infirm and feel it in the beat
Of streaming waters that would tear thee down.
Where is the rest? Oh, not in nature's face,
For her divine revealments and repose
Are only contrast to the craving sting
Of inward agitation. Here at least
Upon this central alpine pinnacle
The weary day arises once again
In all its beauty, sheathed with glossy cloud.
The stars are moving to their still desire:
The pale mist zones one trembling orb: the capes

E.

Are lovely, and their snowy spiral throng

Sharpens in morning; thro' that ample calm

The low fresh fields are hushed in crystal air:

The shining ledges flash: the bordered shales

In rippling specks evolve celestial light,

And glaze the rocks with motion: the light herb

Grasps them, inhaling increase at the sun,

And so endures a season its delight

Of arching skies, so withers. As I gaze,

In silence the innumerable veils

Descend in roseate drift: aspiring shafts

Glister in rose to meet them, till the sun

Is broadly imminent, and changes all.

Then the firm-seated mirror of the morn

Weighs on some lonely flakes becalmed among

The liquid depth unclouded, and the shine

Breaks, tears, and pastures out their streamy spires,

Erasing all their station vein by vein,

Till the great round burns silent and alone,

Ruling his baffled rivals from his seat,

To leave the unfolded interval of Heaven
Silent through all her precincts as a dream.

But what to me the glory and the strong
Emotion? I have wandered through the earth,
And always borne a curse upon my heart,
Darkening the order of celestial change :
So not the mild accord of vernal bird,
So not the deeds that reach us from the dead
To chide our lax endeavour, not the breath
Of some heroic trumpet in the past,
So not the thought that moves us to contend
When life is young with us, from native love
Of motion for itself,—not these, not all
Can draw delight upon a blasted thing.

My road is yonder in the devious vales,
At times it glistens like a silver thread :
At times the mist is kindled as a dust
And sweeps between. So onward, till the end.

The longer pause becomes an agony

That makes this forward toil with all its pain

A preferable evil.   Fall on fall,

The mountain stream has instinct towards the sea,

Her great ulterior rest.   What hope is mine,

To make me wrestle with the flinty bands

That sting my weary footsteps to no goal?

THE APOTHEOSIS OF A TOWN HERO.

THE sacrifice is ended—father, come :
　　Beneath the olives yonder there is rest.
The hymn of consecration and its close
Dwell on my fancy yet : the crowd is poured
About the vacant streets : the garlands droop
On architrave and fluted column-work.
The spiral smoke mounts feebler, and the ash
Is embered in the censer : all is done.
Henceforth the man Dicæus, at whose hand
This city drew such broad prosperity,
Is numbered with the everlasting Great
For lawful worship, hero, demigod,
Guardian for aye of right municipal
In this our native city-commonwealth

Hero is God, my father : but you say
That this same man, who wrought the state such praise,
Was, when he moved among us, much as we ;
Only with greater fixity of will
To make the thing he wished, the thing he did :
And you alone of all this town survive
Who face to face lived with him, man to man.
The times are changed : the hero's stuff is done.
I do not think there will be any more.

You tell me 'nay,' that you and he have trod
Thro' foul and fair together, with no thought
That you were souls unequal, each to each
Conceding, as our common friendships use ;
Allowing small vexations and the need
Of trivial talk for solace on the road :
And now that he is equal with the race
Of heroes, Heracles, or Brasidas
Of age more recent—you a broken man
Declining from the vigour of your time,
And daily losing something of the past.

You loved the man and watched him mount serene

The gradual road of civic eminence.

He spread his hands to glory and it came:

The elements of discord in his eyes

Pealed out their cloudy bolts: the shocks of state

Beat on him like a rampart, and he stood

In that high region, like a thing at rest,

Invulnerably dauntless. At his voice

The city armed or rested: absolute

In council, as a private citizen

He trod our streets and gave his word to all.

He ripened thus his glory, chiefly blest

To leave it, as he left it, full and fair:

For dying, as he died, some worthless man

Had surely gained an honourable grave;

To him, the crowning and immortal close

Of undiminished honour this became,

To die where he had conquered, with a smile,

Under his country's banner as it stood

Upon the alien rampart. At his side

You knelt his ancient comrade, and received
The latest pressure of the strengthless hand,
The recognition of his last regard:
The leader, statesman, he, and you his friend
A nameless soldier in the city's war.

And that you loved the man beyond the taint
And touch of envy, envying but his death,
Rejoicing in his honour: you are old,
My father, now; but this your broken age
Is good in this, that you have seen to-day
What our most narrow season in the light
Forbids the race of man before he sleep—
You have seen a younger generation meet
To consecrate the type of living worth
In your own day, which you had loved, but these
Behold gigantic through the misty years.

ROSAMOND.

H E moved among his captains to the wine,
The revel deepened with the downward day:
By bench and column huge barbarian lengths
Round tankards threw a sprawl of chaining arm
And hugg'd their gleaming poison, with fierce eyes
Fiercer between the draughts.   One leant: one lay:
One thundered out a Rhætian battle-field
Half-cancell'd in the anarchies of time,
Whereon he dealt decision like a god.
One half in shade, gigantic shadow, slept,
And some ill vision writhed his nostril's edge
And made his face a tumult, as his teeth

Ground audibly, and clenched the massive hands.

And one with fewer years and ambered hair

Told all the sweetness of his lady's eyes

To some gray swordsman on his brand declined,

Deaf to the burning words and all the rout,

But gazing with cold orbs on something far

Beyond the banquet and the banquet noise.

And most sat level at the lengthened board,

Intent alone on revel-moving wine.

And royal Alboin feasted, chief of men,

And held his state encanopied beyond

In crimson splendours, like a flushing cloud

Above the secret morning : larger he

And mightier than the congregated peers

Of all the Lombard army : he had drained

Huge draughts Falernian to his idol gods,

Who gave him pleasant seat among a land

Of waters and of summits for his own,

And lovely Pavia to his lordly rest.

And then the fierce and cheating spirit of wine
Made proud his heart. He looked upon his men
And he believed himself invincible,
Till rolling out his arrogant words he said:

'Princes and Leaders of the Lombards, hear,
Have I not led you to a pleasant land?
Who hath withstood our armies for a day?
We conquer all things with a careless hand:
The blast and forward shadow of our tread
Compel the strength of triple-cinctured towns,
And hide their men in marshes: desolate
The streets: their riches ready to our hands.
And now, behold, our large prosperity
Is founded stable as the careless hills
That wind and storm unroot not like their pines.
Much meat is ours in safety till the end
From flocks and cattle in uncounted vales:
What stint of revel when a hundred hills
Are ours, and all their vineyards to our cheer!'

Wisely are we descended to these plains :

In frozen hills what empire? to dispute

Uncouth dominion in the hungry north,

This was the slender wisdom of our sires :

And we are gods to these, that in their day

Did well, as wisdom went, but we are more,

The braver fruitage of a fatter soil.

Their gods have given them rest among their snows,

And conquest to their sons with lordly ease.

I pledge the memory of their silent years :

Have I no nobler vintage than the last,

No choicest warmth of concentrated fire,

No vine-blood rare as gold? For I would crush

The purple essence of Italian heaven

To pledge them in our best since we have thriven.

Nay—while the grateful riot of their praise

Burns in my pulses to a deeper thirst,

I drink it and it trickles to my core—

I feel an evident and conquering god.

I will not pledge them in unmeaning gold,

'The cup shall be more worthy than the praise,

More precious than the wine, a royal bowl:

Bring forth the lordliest beaker of my store,

The skull of Cunimund—here wrought the brain

That planned me frequent death—it holds my wine!

So fall my foes. There is no fitter cup

To pledge our fathers in eternal sleep.

Refill it yet: shall I believe the wine

Has drawn a vengeance-relish from the bone,

Gliding, as love's soft kiss between my lips,

To light a nobler tumult in my heart?

Refill again—go bear it to the Queen,

Bid her rejoice among us with her sire:

Ay, by my country's gods she *shall* rejoice;

Have I not sworn it can I not compel?

Were it the blood of her detested sire,

Shall she not taste a vengeance to *my* foe?'

He ended in a tumult of acclaim

So fierce the wine had stung them to a thirst

Of brutal exultation, cruelties,

And devil-vengeance : but the wiser few

Shuddered and sickly pushed their goblets by,

Waiting the issue.   Helmichis alone,

Who bare the armour of the Lombard King,

Sate with the clouded thunder of his brow

Silent yet ripe to glisten into sound :

So fierce his breathing laboured, towards his brand

His touch went eager fingering out the blade

An inch, but let it linger for the event.

They bore the charnel tankard to the Queen ;

She sate among her ladies at the loom.

Before the beat of nearing steps their laugh

Ceased, as the birds cease music ere a storm.

She glanced surprise upon them, with pressed palms.

She moved not in emotion beautiful,

As beautiful as thought : her gliding eyes

Of resolute azure failed not : some light cloud

Of doubt in floating wrought as light a shade,

And touched the rose confusion of her cheek

To curves that spoke command upon her lip,

One only fleck on her divine repose:

Until she heard the mandate, and beheld

The ghastly token of the hollow brow

She loved so well, and its ignoble use,

Linked with her own constraint most horrible.

Then as a watcher by a summer sea,

With rosy clouds behind it, may perceive

The landscape instant thickened, and white force

Tear down the ripple with an undertone

Of hoarse and ominous mischief, so intense

The large waves cannot lift their mounded rage,

And all the emerald weather's cope serene

Blackens and is transfigured—So her face

Changed and her pale lips trembled: her deep eyes

In tremulous shimmer, counterchanged with glare

Of rushing lights, came wildly: the light hands

Worked, as with deathbed clutches; thro' her frame

One seething shudder's long continuous creep

Convulsive shook her nature to its core.

Nor yet her proud will failed of self-command

In that excessive and tumultous sting

Of pain and bitter wronging keen as death :

One moment and she crushed her weakness down,

And masked unrest with most unnatural calm,

And feigned obedience in her wild revolt

Of love and instinct; she controlled her voice

To speak smooth words ; then with some meek incline

Tenderly raised the skull in filial hands,

And bowed her fair lips meekly to the rim.

But scarcely let the feel of that loathed wine

Moisten upon them : shuddering then she ceased

And murmured faint, 'Let my lord's will be done.'

Yet ere she gave again the cup, she took

Its bony seams upon her lips, and thrice

She kissed it, thrice and closely ; and these went

And bare it to Alboin : she remained

Silent among the silence of her maids,

To weave again with shuddering hands the loom,

And never shed one tear or spake a word,
And a great silence settled in her bower.

But when the pale light strengthened out its day,
Remorse on Alboin fell when that ill cheer
Of wine had left him, and he knew her wrong
Was bitter, most malignant: since her soul,
Proud in its least obedience, must recoil
From that excessive test in burning shame.
And the King thought to make her some amends,
But being proud endured not to unsay
The tumid folly of his feasting hours:
And, tho' he wished, said nothing for the day;
So left the wrong to fester unatoned.

But she arose from slumber's restless mock
Of raging dreams: one purpose of revenge
Possessed her life: all other thought became
Vassal to one endeavour's sole command.
Then sent she forth and summoned Helmichis;

To her imperial summons he repaired,

And guessed the import of her sending now:

And when he came she looked into his eyes,

And took his hand and held it as she spake:

'Dost thou remember the old days that were,

Before this King had placed me at his side

By right of conquest when my father fell.

No maiden choice was mine but to obey.

The mock of insolent conquest I assumed

Detested queendom at a victor's hand:

Surely I owe my tyrant lord much love.

But when I dwelt a girl with Cunimund,

And moulded fancies in my father's halls,

One came and whispered love, and that was thou:

Those days are dust and Alboin came between,

He made an orphan where he sought a bride,

And rooted out my race to speed his vows:

And fancied, as he dragged me at his wheels,

Submission was a nobler thing than love.

'I was his queen, and I endured this curse

Some years without complaint. I will endure

No longer: patience falters at the last.

Last night he planned strange insult at his wine,

Disgrace no daughter ever bare and throve

Thereafter and forgave it: such fierce shame

As makes submission infamy, and tears

Allegiance from the empty name of wife.

I have sworn a stedfast oath that he shall die.

Why should this tyrant trample on more souls,

Swell like a god in his impunity?

And if those former vows of thine endure,

If change has been as silent in thy heart

As mine through all the turmoil of these years,

Thine, thine shall be the hand to make me free.

I know thee brave, I know thou lovedst me once,

When this is done thou shalt not question long

If then I loved again. I cannot fear

Refusal when I look upon thy face

Heroic and recount my utter wrong!'

She ended, and he promised her desire:

What could he else? such power upon his soul

Wrought thro' her words and earnest pleading eyes.

Meantime, secure in his imperial halls,

Alboin feared no vengeance for her wrong.

DÆDALUS.

THE craftsman Dædalus, the slave of kings,
    Artificer of nations, instrument
Of fools that use his fingers, and refuse
The shelter of their gates, the drift and mock
Of royal whim and civic insolence,
The man of ready brain and cunning hand—
It has not come to much this life of mine.

Yet once again an exile: there it lies
This city which I peopled with my brain,
And fed with water from the hills, and changed
Their hovels into marble palaces.

And carved them gods to worship with the eyes
Of mortal beauty: this is my reward.
This petty tyrant thunders like a Zeus
And thrusts me out on surmise, with excuse,
'Forsooth his craft is dry, and we have reapt
His brain to stubble: let him pack and flee,
Lest he should flout us with his benefits.'

Was it for this that I have pondered out
The forces of the earth, and made man strong
Beyond his puny fibre to remove
Some mountain like the Titans? As a god,
Creating power in new development,
I seated man the regent of the world:
Whom I had found a cowering slave, beneath
The cattle in endurance, walking blind
Among the helps and wonders at his feet.

It is the curse of wisdom to endure
The scorn of fools that use us when their need

Is ended; then the brutish herd accounts
Intelligence as treason to the rule
Of universal blindness. I have seen
The noisy birds that peck to death their kind
If one of lighter plumage should intrude
Among their even blackness; typing thus,
How men reject the spirits that presume
To leave their age behind them, and uphold
Attentive faces to the purple light
That thickens where the later sun shall tread.

For he that smooths the daily lives of men
By mere material comfort must upraise
The moral nature: as the home the man.
I have done this, have built their houses firm
And beautiful; so taught them to provide
A better food with fire: to reap their crops,
And carve or plane the fissile woods at hand.
In softer wools I clothed them, and have drawn
The flax in closest fibre. At my hand

The sea-shell rendered up intenser stain ;
For colour works with form an equal power,
Subduing and refining thro' the world.

I must not pause to murmur, or the night
Shall take me on the summits: I would live
And reap, in spite of envy, the delight
Of new creation for itself; beyond
I know there is no recompence: my work
Is excellent or worthless in itself ;
And I am weak to murmur if to-day
Is chary of its praise, the after-time
Will set me right.   If the blind mole reprove
The glory of the dawn shall nature cease
Her radiance for his blindness.   I will on,
And scorn to stint my effort till the end.
The gods, that made me what I am, will keep
My record and avenge me on this age.
In Hellas there are towns enough to prove

My use and my rejection. Chance shall guide

My footsteps: in our energy we live,

And all the rest is dream and accident.

THE LAMENT OF PHAETHON'S SISTERS.

THE short-lived crocus bring and moly bloom,
   Sweet incense gum and odorous cedar burn,
With roses we will strew his sepulchre,
A vernal wreathing for a royal tomb.

   Ill-fated, most presumptuous brother mine,
The gleaming chariot couldst thou dare ascend
To guide the sun-steeds, mortal charioteer?

   Our father, he the unapproachable,
Phœbus, the lord of Delos, in his sphere
Eternally surrounded by the flakes

Of awful glory—frowned at thy request,
Nor yet denied it : rashly hath he sworn
By that infernal river, which alone
Can bind the ageless gods in their despite,
That he will hear the first boon of his son.

Ah, ye our father's horses, steeds of day,
Could ye destroy this brother, to our tears?
Hence shall we no more bring you golden food,
Divine, ambrosial barley : now no more
Our hands shall love to sleek your proud necks down,
No more our wandering fingers comb your manes :
Ye have betrayed him, to our utter woe.

Then sped the bolt of Zeus, eternal King,
An irresistible vengeance on thy head,
To scorch thy wretched life, and thou wast hurled
Out on the realms of space, as falls a grain
Of sand to sound the ocean infinite.
Immeasurable depth, and falling still.

Three days among the stars, and falling still,
Blackened with lightning, towards the misty earth.

Until we found thee by the river here;
Thy beauty scarred; with sad distorted face:
Our love alone had known thee in that hour.

Here in the genial bosom of the mould,
Enswathed with costly cerement, choose his rest:
And we sad watchers, by its sacred rim,
Upon the crystal river weep long tears,
And thick as amber rain our sorrow down.

And sigh, as yonder margin poplars sigh,
That droop above the sedges their sere leaves;
With these in unison shall moan the flood
A dirge for thee, beloved one, brother mine,
Ill-fated, most ill-fated brother mine.

JAMES AND MARY.

BESIDE a furzy common patched with sand,
  An ancient mansion stood, a piebald heap
Of blackened oak and plaster: in the days
Of queenly Bess a hall, a farmstead now.
Here Martha Bruce for many years abode,
A widowed mother with a single child,
Mary a comely blossom of eighteen.

  Now Martha, ere she fell in widowhood,
Had in her cares of wifedom fretful grown:
A grievance-searching nature hers, most keen
To guage and probe the petty rubs and thorns

Of household custom : dwelling on her cares,
She bred them for herself from carelessness
And want of system ; then on these complained
In needless-fretful whining, till she made
The mote annoyance bulge a beam of wrong,
And half believed herself an injured drudge,
The very model of a wife ill-used.

And thus she found her trouble for herself
By faults of nature part, of nurture more :
Forsooth she had been delicately bred,
A yeoman's daughter upon gentry's verge,
Taught that to move in homely usefulness,
To touch a pan or darn a stocking end,
Were loss of caste : the lady must not toil ;
And the more helpless the more lady she.
And thus the girl grew, till she came to wed,
Environed with a draff gentility :
And when she wedded with a poorer man
She started on the test of married days

With slender stock of foresight; soon to fail,
And sour herself and make a curse of home,
Alternative in shrewing and in tears.
And, after years, her goodman chanced to die;
She, left with narrow store and one weak child,
Held barely on the farm as best she might
Unthrifty, cankered with penurious days,
While still she gave her want the fiercer sting
With jarring discontents, and evil thoughts
Against her richer neighbours in the land.

And she would prate to Mary as she grew,
Filling the child with vainness and conceit,
How ne'er another lass in all the shire
Could touch her Mary's beauty by a league.
And she could tell, nay, well enough she knew,
Mary's sweet face should drive the neighbour lads
Half mad in time: but she was not for these.
Nay, but she hoped her child would bring her ease,
And come to marry in a wealthy house,

And comfort her old mother's latter days
In sunshine and the honour of her name.

But to the fair face, dreaming on the world
Of future wonder and the things to be,
The rolling years came slowly, till the time
Had shaped her woman and had overborne
Her girlhood. Then the mother looked at her
And thought, ' My wish sights haven in this child.
My still endeavour all these eighteen years
Has fruited richly. I shall see good days
And lay my bones in honourable rest.'

But westward of the heath by some hours' ride,
James Bolton lived, half farmer and half squire,
Florid, fair-built, some twenty-four years old :
Who rode his hunters : kept his park of deer,
A small one : owned some land and rented more.
He, from the hunt thrown out one winter eve,
Pushed meditative homewards with loosed rein ;

And chanced on Mary leaning near a well

To lift her pitcher: in whose gentle eyes

He read a power that seemed to clothe in light

The gray lane with its bare and soughing twigs

Of leafless hazel: and his horse drew up

Guessing the rider's mind. But James's blood

Came at a leap in crimson to his face,

Deep as the red leaves showering from the eaves

Of cottage trailers: somewhat less she blushed;

As the warm west answers the eastern glow

At sunrise matching with a fainter rose.

And so they dwelt confusedly: but he

Grasping suggestion, with a quickened brain,

From the mid flutter of his heart, devised

To feign a thirsty pretext for delay,

So perhaps to speak a word or change a glance.

And she, how could she else? with some faint smile

Willingly gave the bright wave of the well

Caught from its source and trickling now no more

In prison walls, and reached it, near as fair

As she, whose story in the Church is read,

The mother of the favoured Israel.

So Mary stood: he leaning from his steed

Forgot his thirst in gazing o'er the rim

Upon the giver, and, so ending, thanked:

And with some trivial sentence interchanged

Past on and homewards; only to return

With the gray light of the succeeding days,

And wait beside the freshet till she came.

Till it grew custom and they settled hours

Of frequent tryst; and love newborn resumed

The millionth time upon two wondering hearts

His ancient empire; trustful love as young

As when the first pale lovers moistened eyes,

And trusted vows were everlasting stuff

And passion's lease eternal.

                  So the time

Wore: and the mother, in short-sighted zeal,

For Mary dared not tell her yet of James

From some vague awkwardness and half in fear,

Dinned in the daughter's ear perpetual praise

Of one rich miller in a neighbour vale.

Her very model of a son-in-law,

This miller with his solemn face inane,

Broad-cheeked, and well-to-do, and middle-aged,

Easily natured, patient to be led :

Slow in his speech, nor rash to overflow

In glancing topic or colloquial fence.

He, in a mooning fondness for the girl,

Would sit, on drowsy Sunday afternoons,

On the same parlour chair, in staid routine

Of an accredited courtship, much besunned

With bland maternal smiles and meaning looks.

But Mary sat unmoved with wearied face :

For duller seemed the good man than a day

That drips without a stint from dawn to dusk.

And so he came by clock-work and withdrew

The same to a minute, phrasing his farewell

Upon a constant formula : nor dreamt

In his thick hide that Mary wished him gone
Ere he had passed the door: and, week by week,
Heavily amorous, still he came and came,
And took his courtship as his Sunday beef,
Equally stolid, and with both content.

But, after that James Bolton sought her heart,
On Mary loathing towards that other grew:
Where hardly she had borne him from the first
Outright she hated now, and gave to James
A deeper tenderness: so time went on.

At length the miller on a Sunday noon
Walked with the mother in the orchard grass;
Where, plucking heart with prefatory hems,
He told her there and then, 'that, on advice,
For folks had told him he had courted now
The right time to an ell, who knew the best
How such things should be with a thriving man,
Who paid his way, and might, but he cared not

For such things—and worse men had done it too—
Subscribe himself Esquire. Well, it were best,
Since he should wed her daughter, to agree
The how and when, and clench the matter soon.
The girl seemed shy at times : young girls *were* shy :
Time set that right : it suited him as well.
He did not want a girl to droop and pine,
And swear she loved him fifty times a-day,
Fierce tinder soon burnt out. The best of wives
Were they that wed without the trash of hearts
And lover nonsense. All that folks required
To rub on well together thro' the world
Came after marriage.'

      This he blurted out
In puffs unevenly, unusual length
Of verbiage for his silence. Martha gave
Joyful assent, and promised for her child
All should be smooth and settled in a week.

Then Martha told her daughter, and the girl

Looked scared, but answered nothing for the night;
Nor would the mother press her further then.
So Mary slipt in silence to her rest;
But ere she slept she wrote to James, and told
How things went ill against their love at home:
And how her mother hurried on the match
She hated, and she knew not what to do.

On James his trouble thickened as he read,
For need of action came in unripe hour,
Ere he had settled purpose with himself.
He feared his mother likewise; who abode
And kept his house with him, and watched her son
With jealous and maternal tyranny.
She, daughter of a county family,
Had ruled her goodman straitly till his death,
Quelling his free-will with superior birth
And right assumed of territorial pride:
And, since this sway bore weaker on the son,
She ever strove, by straining it the more,

To brace her tottering frail prerogative.

Thus, to sustain her ground, she came to feel

Past reason querulous on imagined slight

And faintest contradiction: and James knew

That all her heart, as all her pride, was set

To match him with a slip of some great squire,

Whose race had held their acres, sire to son,

Since rose with rose contended, in a chain

Of proud, obscure, and dull gentility.

Now James had wrote to Mary he would come

The morrow; so he turned the question round

Thro' all that day and half a restless night

In sleep, that came, more hateful than unrest,

To feign distorted shadows of his thought.

And so with light he rose, and unrefreshed

Rode out across the meadows, crushing down

His care with motion in the whistling airs

Of morning: and he rested not his steed

Until he found her by the lisping well

Pallid as he was pale, and in her eyes
He read the crisis of his life was come.

Then she, 'Alas, my own and not my own!
I tremble in the presence of this hour,
Which parts or binds us all our doom of days
Till we are cold in earth, and summer-time
Is one with winter on the pulseless heart.
We plant weak vows eternal, else unroot
The slender threads which held us in a soil
Of rich delusion. Thine, O love, to choose:
On thee self-doubtful leaning I withhold
My wavering judgment : yet in one resolve
Most resolute am I, that if mistrust
Or fleck of unsure purpose touch thy wish
To cast in hand with mine this earthly time—
I will begone and see thy face no more,
And bear it patiently, as bear I can :
And better thus, than in my autumn days
To hang a clog about the neck I love
When this poor cheek has worn its freshness by.'

She faltered, ending thus, and dimmed his sight :
Yet at his brain, while moister grew his eyes,
A selfish instinct came. As one at bay,
Environed with self-wrought perplexities,
Sees some escape, unhoped for, thrust at him,
And, good or evil, grasps it—So with James,
Chancing on sudden outlet, eager flashed
Suggestion to ensure it :

                     ' When I came,
And found you, Mary, listening in soft light,
Strong love thrust out all hazards to conclude
Thy fate and mine together. But thy words,
Children of wisdom, wisely have imposed
Some rein of caution on the sudden heart,
That rushes blindly to its end, with guide,
Save heated fancy, none. I now reverse
My former mind : I see that wait we must :
Wait in no rash endeavour to foresee
The sequel, or precipitate the close :
And yours to bend this mother to delay

Our stolid miller's suit, too mean to raise
Much anger, else abhorred : allege, you can,
A peck of girlish reasons. Love, take heart;
Be, love demands it, in entreaty brave ;
And all shall prosper nobly, when I win
My mother down to reason from her pride.'

And so they kissed and parted. But James rode
Homewards with loosened rein : no ease at heart :
Vext that he had not acted fair and well.
So, pricking on the faster to beat down
The chafing thought, he took across the fields,
To slice an angle from the road, and cleared
The fences in his line : but at the third
The horse, who rose not, crushing thro' the stakes
Rolled on his rider, whom some ploughmen came
And found, to bear him homewards sense-bereft.

But James was long in fever from his fall,
And him his mother tended. But mischance

Brought in his coat the letter to her hand,

Last writ of Mary, when they brought him in

Helpless and stunned. She read it, and long days

The mother watched him, scheming to unweave

The love this letter taught. Some comfort this,

His illness, bad in most, was good in this

That she might plot unthwarted : and she held,

All means were holy and a mother's right

To stave her son from this perpetual shame

Of mating low : for all her thought was blind

And warped with narrow county pride ; and chief

She feared her spinster sisters in their hall

Lined with the canvas faces of past squires,—

Great squires, each in his narrow walk supreme,

Lords of the hind and acres at their gate,

They drank, bred, hunted their allotted time,

Then gave the parish-church one hatchment more.

So, from fierce dread this match might come about

In her despite, when James was up and sound.

The mother stooped to guilt: and first she penned

In James's hand close-mimicked some vague lines,

Hinting on doubts to Mary, half-grown fears,

To let her gently down, and pave the road:

So prelude in her final forgery

The key-note of her plot: this last she sent

A week in rear. From James the writing ran

In purport crafty, 'That, in deepest pain,

Tortured he wrote with all perplexity—

He was not master of the course of things,

He least could guide them: he had broached his love

For Mary to his people one by one:

Had tried remonstrance, all persuasion—drops

On granite—"Wed he must if wed he would

Beneath him; he was master of himself.

They could not stay his wiving, nor could he

Constrain *them*—and on this their mind was firm—

To change a single nod with his vile choice

Caught from the milk-pail.'" The insidious hand

On Mary laid decision what was best,

Assured she could but answer and release
James of all faith henceforward. As indeed
Came the reply of Mary, penned in tears,
'But blaming James in nothing, with a prayer
That he might find some worthier than herself
To make him happy at a future day.
Nor must James fret about her : she would choose
Mayhap in time an equal when this dream
Had faded, one whose mother should not blush
To call her daughter—ending with farewell.'
And when this came the mother had good heed
To intercept it from the sick man's hand.
So in her scheme she prospered, still in dread
Lest James should move about again too soon
And crush her web to nought.

     But that day month
The pale sad Mary, crushed with evil days
And goaded by her mother, morn and noon,
Wedded the heavy miller, and so passed
Beyond the land, to pore in after years

On what had been, and train a patient heart
In one dull round of loveless duty's sphere.

But James, who mended slowly, chanced to read
The County Herald, lighting on the news:
And for a space the ceiling and the walls
Swam round him, sick and stunned.   He giddily rose,
And strove to dress and dash aside his pain;
But on him came his weakness and prevailed,
As clearer flashed conviction of his full
And utter desolation.   Could he mend
An hour of her irrevocable doom
Now were his strength at fullest?   Lost as dead
Was Mary now: could strong despair unknit
Life-woven vows, the goodman from his wife?
And, if he moved, of bad should worse ensue
To Mary full as wretched as himself,
If he knew right, in this thrice-loathed result
Of motherly compulsion.   Fool and blind
To waver two months since: then blindly ride

A break-neck course in spleen : thus men lost all.

He wished his neck *had* broken : this had spared

All self-reproach, much bitterness of time

Hereafter, and the sting of wasted chance.

He must not even see her, but sit still,

In forced inaction dribbling out his days

With trivial occupation as they came.

So wore his life away; till at the last

In apathy or weakness, or in both,

He wedded as his mother bade him wed,

And never knew her guilty till his grave.

NIOBE.

BEHOLD I am the mother of all woes,
  An isolation on a living earth
Of creatures meting love and loved again:
There is no moving life that loves me left.

  I dreamt that there was mercy with the gods,
And like a child I dreamt it: for I hold
The adder largely pitiful to these,
He kills not but in hunger and defence
And not for pastime: the brave Delian's bolt
Prefers the innocent: he draws on man
Behind his hedge of immortality
Secure of counter aim: trim courage this.
And noble exploit were it to besmear
Some widow's cheeks with sorrow: to destroy

Her orphan brood and quell the beaming eye:

To trample trust and youth in dust and shame.

I knew not this your right omnipotence.

I had but heard that man's adversity

Was something for your contemplative choir

To gaze upon with dull incurious eyes,

As on a curious picture new no more.

These gods have watched so many thousands die,

Have learnt so well each phase of human pain,

That, to relieve their leisure, they must plan

Yet more ingenious torture: since to slay

At once were feeble pastime, stale and old:

Stale as that old, old prayer, monotonous,

For something which these men have Mercy named:

A word forbidden in the shining halls,

Or with your dynasty of recent gods

Disused and changed for Vengeance.

     Art thou King,

O Zeus, who drowzest on thy dappled clouds?

Thou spreadest hugely on the wearied clouds:

Dost wake to murder, as a prince to hunt,
Clearing the fumes of nectar round thy brain
With thunder tossed in pastime on our towns?
Tear up the yellow harvests with thy brand,
And cheat the hungry mouths of foodless men:
Mock them with famine: let the slaves lick up
The leavings of thy storm: some patch of maize
Outstands the scathing bluster: the rained brooks
Are drink enough, and draff and shards content
The aches of famine till men cease, and pass
Under the night to plague the gods no more:
Their dole of tears is wept: they fear no cold.

Ye thralls of meanest vengeance, tyrant gods,
Who mar the sacred nature in her fruit,
Who relish all disorder and unfaith,
Whence your authority that frame such deeds?
Ill power that put you stronger than our lives.
But not your scorn or anger can bereave
The freedom of the breast, that bears about

Innate rebellion to your craven powers.

Ye cannot silence the pale lips, that hurl

The birthright of their protest in the teeth

Of domineering wrong they cannot stay,

Since some blind fate has seated wrong supreme.

Triumph in wrong, thou race of Zeus: the earth,

Is at thy feet for carnage: run thy day

Of tyranny, and turn thy careless eyes

To other desolation: there is food

For thine immortal arrows otherwhere,

And children fair as mine in peaceful homes

For new destruction: slacken not thy hand,

Lest men grown happy say thy rule is done.

It is a fruitful race this breed of man,

And thrives by thinning: victims will not fail:

To spare, lest this should be, were idiot fear:

Not thy full malice shall extirpate all.

But O ye elder race of gentler gods,

Whom these have bound in darkness, whom the voice
Of lamentation at the upstart Kings
Adjures as only worthy to command;
As only gods in deed, tho' these prevail.
Our hope is towards you chained beneath the world:
We whisper that you are not conquered yet:
That not in record human or divine
Was evil yet eternal: tyranny
Is doomed as soon as born, and bears about
The seeds of sure destruction, from the germ
Coeval with its growth; and doomed its rule
However long the respite of its fall.

Arise ye Titans then, for these are weak,
Rend out your adamantine chains, and shake
The mountains from your limbs, infirm no more
To yield your ancient seats: resume that might
Which girdled round the world ere these had drawn
Their baby milk, and crush them from the sky.
Arise ye Titans and avenge my tears.

THE SALE AT THE FARM.

I TRUST the worst is over with this sale.
  The old place had a strange look in the crowd :
The jostling and the staring and the creak
Of shuffled feet, the public laugh sent round,
The hammer's clink, the flippant auctioneer,
Number on number lengthening out the day :
Familiar things dishonoured, like old friends
Set up on high to scorning fools : and then
The ache of loss, and some dull sense that they
Would sell me last by parcels, till the dusk
Drew, in December sleet, and all were gone :
And this old wreck bowed at my drooping fire

In gathered shade unfriended and alone.
Bare walls and fixtures here: thus ends the tale.

George Barnes, the thriving farmer, warpt and shrunk
And naked to the bite of wind and wave.
On the blank threshold of his eightieth year,
Ripe for the parish union or the grave.
The man whose name was clean and word was sure
Dishonoured: pattern farmer of the squire,
The farm of gapless hedge and pasture clean
Without a rush: I, broken, the safe man
As England's bank for credit? when old Groves,
Who never paid a punctual rent, scrapes on,
With his lean kine, like Egypt's plagues, at grass
Where sprouts one blade of herbage to the score
Of rushes stubbled close as urchin quills.

Ye idle sons, ye false and idle sons,
A bitter ending to my careful years
Ye have devised me in your lurcher pride:

Why should ye make me homeless at the last?

Ye knew that thrift had raised the labouring man

A fruitful farmer: your vain wits forgot

The two-roomed cottage of your schooling years;

A labourer's sons to ape at gentlemen:

To drink and racket like the careless heirs

Of noble acres, race and ride to hounds;

Fine clothes, French wines, ill comrades from the town:

And then to come and tell me, that I shamed

Your worships by still working with my men

In these old fields that bought you all your show.

Meanwhile your farms went wrack in bailiffs' hands,

Ye saw to nothing, stinted not, spent on:

Ye never held a plough or bound a sheaf:

Lord, I have seen you ride on harvest days,

Among the smoking reapers, spruce and cool,

Be-gloved and Sunday-coated, vain and gay

As weedy poppies among honest grain.

And so these ran their tether out like lords,

While loan and credit lasted, and one year

Had back to bear the burden of the last
And pass it to another with its own.
And so they ran their folly to the lees,
And borrowed deeper till their flash studs failed,
And I to save some shreds of our good name
Sat down at four-score beggared—so it runs.

With nought I started and with nothing end :
For I and my old dame in our young days—
Kind soul, she's best in churchyard from these tears—
From her brisk needle and my labourer's wage
Contrived to scrape a little, coin by coin,
Albeit hungry mouths were in our nest
Of growing children, and the wages low.
And after hours I wrought a patch of waste
Into a garden : many helps are found
By those who seek them like midsummer bees
Making the long days longer, and our store
Grew under wary watching like a child.
We bought a cow to pasture in the lanes ;

And since occasion helps the helpful man,

The squire's head woodman failing, I came in

Till there was picked another to their mind.

And since I felled as much at lower wage,

And since the bailiff gave me sturdy praise,

And since the squire could light on no one else,

They were content to leave this as it stood,

And no one came above me, so I throve.

And after years a leasehold farm fell in,

The homestead ruinous and the land undrained,

No specious venture; for the dribbling term

Had thrown it lastly to a needy man

Who almost starved upon it, a poor soul

Crippled with ague and consuming sloth.

Thus an ill name, the fault of his neglect,

Clung to the farm and scared the applicants.

Till, last the steward bating of his rents,

I closed the venture, now to stand or fall.

My savings scarce could stock it at the first

All was awry, and, rood by rood, the land

With stubborn pains reclaimed from careless years,

Set me afield before the sleeping sun.

I dyked the solid marls with sturdy zeal,

Slaved like ten ploughmen in November dwift,

And bent the stubborn fallows to my will.

But at the full fall of the leaf there came

A bitter season in my second year

With sickness to our cattle, and with pain

We barely weathered through it to the spring.

Once safely through, large store of better days

Succeeded, and above our heads the sun

Of prosperous labour held an even noon.

And days of golden plenty flowed in toil

That set an honest relish on the day,

And gleamy tints by day's unstormy fall

Gave equal promise of to-morrow calm.

And when our children and our store increased

I took this larger farm, reputed first

In all the township. I have made its name

Lose nothing in my keeping, year by year;
I made its good yet better; and I throve.

And as these sons grew men, I said, 'the boys
Shall each be started well and have their prime
Unfettered with the clogs that kept me down.
If my tough arms and purpose seat me here,
Why should I toss these troubles to the lads
Of my probation? they shall till their own,
And owe their labour to no man beside,
Lords of their honest strength and sinew sure.'

And spoke unwisely: 'tis a perilous thing
To give a lad some choice of idleness,
And plenty carved too ready at his hand.
Better as I was: this I knew not then:

And as each son came twenty and a year.
Three sons I set them in three farms to thrive,
No farmers better started in the shire.

And thus they have repaid me, like sour weeds
That steal the room and nurture of the grain
Under whose shade and sufferance they are sprung,
And, though they strike no root themselves, contrive
To choke and waste it wholly at the last.

Alas, I erred in being generous.
I could detect no failings in my own :
I thought their hearts were right because their limbs
Were moulded fair, and light was on their face,
The rosy maskings of a feeble core.
And, one by one, they failed from off the land,
Selfish, unstable, vain, and slothful boys.
See these have dragged me down, and thought no
        shame
To link an old man's ruin to their own,
If so they could push back a little while
Their imminent destruction, and secure
Some paltry furlough for their evil ways.
They thought it all the same to strip me now

Or wait to wrangle at my monument.

What matter if my few remainder years

Be comfortably furnished, or commended

To parish charity ? old age is dull:

A dotard could not taste much difference.

I lodged as ill before I made your gold :

But your nice senses are another thing,

They shall not lack full flush of delicates.

Shall gentlemen be shortened of their ease

While the old clod has yet a coat to lose ?

Ay me, these troubles and this weary day

Have loosed my tongue unduly, and revealed

Much grievance better sealed in silent shame.

I am so old no wound can hurt me long.

The future smooths to one both good and blame :

They were my own that wrought their father's fall,

My own, tho' sinning, and these bitter words

Are wrongly spoken by a father's tongue.

Comfort is sure and silence in the grave,

I can abide the bitter interval,

As short as sour, that holds me from my rest.

This desolation and these naked walls

Are seen no longer, for the light is past

From these dead embers: so when I am dead

My thought will dwell no more on any cares.

THE STRANGE PARABLE.*

TOWARDS noon it left me in the sun's full glare.

It shook the habitation of my soul,

And rending sped upon the void. But I,

Albeit my pain was ended, seemed to crave

A necessary presence, and an old

Subsistence of unrest, accustomed long.

The langour and the vacancy of change

Replaced the antagonistic element,

That gave a substance to my life erewhile,

And stung the native energies from sleep

By mere resistance. This had ending now :

The ferment and the tyranny withdrawn,

St. Luke xi. 24.

The agony's vibration smoothed in calm
Left me a painless thing without a soul.

And I fared forth beneath the skies alone
Without a will to guide me, like a drift
In automatic motion; all my life
Chaotic, nerveless now.

      Some influx strove
Of barren dread beside my stagnant heart;
There fear, in dearth of purpose, substitute
And dream of purpose, ruling in her room
Her seat and vacant function.

       So I fared.
Along the arid roots of battered crags,
The flags of yawning heights, the summit shales,
My purpose drave to wander; I abhorred
The oozy footings of the plashy reeds,
The meadows rank with juicy undermath:
And chief I hated those lean wisps of fire
That crowd the peat-tarns nightly, or by gleams

Of wavering twilight; here in festered rank
The winter-sodden bullrush : here the fangs
Of rotten héath in purple blooming cleave
The trembling edges of the emerald floor.
And still I wandered on and yet no peace :
And still I paced the uplands dry and drear :
And still the curse was burning at my heart.

Then to myself I spake and spake with heed,—
The isolation and the restless feet
Of Cain are mine for ever. Shall I choose
Perpetual chaos? Surely I shall cease
If I return not. Pain erewhile was peace.
But this is desolation as the grave ;
The gloom in bitter silence spreads before ;
The moveless drifts are ruled along the verge ;
Above, the ebon vapour's bosomed waves
Lean from the wind, and waver towards their rest.

And I with heedful steps devised return,

My slow blood sick with weariness and strung
To horrible emotion. The sheer slabs
Of granite stung my foot-fall; when the ranks
Of precipice and foreland, crushed and piled
With shocks of desolation, wore in scorn
The violet even on their blasted spires.

What then sustained me through ? no hand of heaven.
The greedy chasm refused me : at my tread
The loosened snows yell downwards, ere my feet
Have made two onward steps. The crazy shales
On lips abysmal hold me by an inch
Of crumbling from the silence and the void—
At last the plain, O God : the bitter heights
Are whistling long behind. This rooted flower
Comes on me like the voices of my friends—
There is my place, last of the level plain :
The mist had masked it wholly, yet I know
The faintest border of the filmy wall ;
And nearer, nearer drawn, my wish is deed.

Ay me, returning, this is no return.

The core of desolation and no rest.

Empty and swept and garnished, I have found

A grave, no home, a blight, a solitude,

And I am lonelier here than on the void.

So went I forth, and took unto my need

Seven former comrades in the naked walls;

They came and dwelt there, souls that mock the light

And banter with the melancholy time,

Unheeding the to-morrow; drowning sense

Of foresight down; contented there to hold

A grim carousal with a staring death

And imminent destruction: but the dwift

And end I know not: this at least I know,

That man with men must change his words or die.

And this I know, man is not man alone,

Dowered with the curse of sociability,

Source of his sinning. Life is aching fret,

And bitter prying through the secret doors

Of future, and stern wrestling with unrest,

Some void of unattainment palling all.

And this I know, relapse is worse than sin

Original; ay me, what help is mine?

THE NAIAD.

RIVER of mine, dear source and parent stream,

    Thy daughter loves upon thy lucid edge

To dream away the summer, and entwine

Thy lilies in her locks the long day thro'.

No sister naiad mine to take delight

Among thy ripples with me, nor beguile

The lazy silence with alternate song.

I am alone with nature and my sire.

    How sweet recumbent by thy gleamy rims

To watch this azure Iris floating out

Her curtained petals in the rosy dawn.

To catch the tender murmur of the sedge
Rising and bending in the cloven stream,
With all its hoary blooms just crisp with wind.
The pastimes of a lonely nymph are these,
Not undelightful days of pensive calm:

There is a cavern where I love to sleep,
With reedy echoes slumberous at its mouth,
And overgrown with fern leaves intricate;
The bees are rustling thro' it all day long,
And drop on drop an amber rillet falls.
No mortal eye has seen my secret nest.

Thence I behold the pastoral vale and meads
Fostered for ever by my father's wave.
Thence in mysterious morning I have heard
Delicious music far and faint: its notes
Float lost in sleepy vales and seem the flute
Of some immortal, viewless in deep woods.
Striving with silence thro' an Orphic fall

Of melody.   Beyond, the piny steep

Exhales a golden vapour, and between

The long-drawn foldings of its sacred vales

A foremost temple-porch aërial, set

On purple cliff wine-dark with granite scars.

I listen as the throbbing music dies,

And find another impulse at my heart.

Its mighty weird prevails against my peace

Destroying god-like calm, and makes me feed

On future like a mortal, with the dreams

Of earthly love, unmeet divine repose

That knows not sorrow.

               Will no hero come?

Either beneath the tremulous arch of eve,

Or thro' the burning dews of sacred morn,

And fold me on his heart, and weave me tales

Of high achievement, how he braved and slew

The dragon in his fastness? Of great wars,

Like old Titanic conflict with the gods,

Wherein his arm had wrestled strong as they.

Then should I love him as he told, and waste
My thirsty soul in fervour on his lips;
For I am here alone and cumbered down
With lonely and unloved divinity.
Sweet is this nature, dear my parent stream :
I love the velvet hills, and joy to hear
The inarticulate music of the earth :
And this calm mind immortal, weighing all
In contemplation and uneager rest,
Is very sweet: why ask this toil of love ?
Nay, love is more than these, and these with love
Are more delicious.

       Father mine, reclined
On thy cold urn, whose everlasting flow
Shall make the riper harvest and enrich
Innumerable kingdoms, seer and sire,
Canst thou unroll the mists across my fate,
And read if I am lonely evermore?
I love thee well, but thy love is not all :
There is a something sweeter yet to be.

DANIEL BEFORE BELSHAZZAR.

WHY have ye led me to this impious hall?
  Thy face, O King, is altered from the joy
Of feasting, and thy mighty ones no more
Carouse, but mutely tremble: blank their eyes
As yonder idiot faces carved in stone
For worship. Hath God spoken at the last?
Patient too long, O God, thou speakest now
To trace a flaming sentence on the wall
Full in the staring of those idols' eyes.
The secret words, O King, thou canst not read.

Nor find interpretation of their fear.

If I declare the writing it shall make

Your feast as dust before you: yonder wine

Shall burn your lips as poison from the cups

Of hallowed gold, whose desecrated use

Hath drawn a vengeance from the eternal King

Of angels down.

      Why should I read alone!

Where are thy wise Chaldeans? Theirs the craft

To read the faces of the silent stars,

Assuring smooth dominion to thy pride:

They change the map of the eternal heaven

Into a lying oracle. Behold

The writing: let them read it: there is store

Of gold and purple for their ready lies,

At such a needful time why are they dumb?

Or, if these fail, make incense to your gods,

Sweet odours, more libation: in your hour

Of prosperous feast they heard your hymns of praise;

And now they must requite their worshippers

For adoration : surely they can save,

For they are gods indeed, not wood or stone.

Behold I am a stranger, and alone

Amid the pride of Babylon : my race,

The children of captivity, were led

From Judah by thy father in his war,

Mean captives of the sword ; and who am I

To stand alone amid thy thousand lords,

And read thee to thy face the words of fear ?

And yet, O King, the writing is not hard :

Search out the haughty annals of thy reign,

For thy recorded empire must ensure

This sequel, surely as night draws the day.

To godless pride there is but one result,

And he who bears himself against high God,

Dooms in that hour his own devoted head.

Thy gifts be to thyself and not for me.

Let other reap reward, but I will none.

Shall I presume to barter recompence

If 1 interpret this divine decree ?

The prophet is no merchant of his craft.

Nor sells his inspiration.   Learn and hear.

Who gave thy father majesty beyond

The nations in his glory ! Whose right arm

Clothed him with terrible fear, and set the necks

Of alien kings beneath his wrathful feet ?

Who gave thy sire his conquest and his throne ?

Who built secure dominion round his rest,

And made him King indeed : a King to slay

Or keep alive the nations as he chose,

To cancel or establish with his nod !

The most high God, the King of kings, gave all,

And prospered in thy father's hand a time

His delegated sceptre that he throve :

Until his heart was lifted in his pride,

And God eternal heard his impious joy.

For thus the King had spoken as he walked

For pleasure on his palace-roof, to view

His large metropolis beneath his feet—

'Is not this city Babylon the great,

Which I have builded for my realm's abode,

The house of all my kingdom, founded sure

As an eternal empire in the might

Of my great glory; this majestic work

For my continual honour till the end?'

But while the word was in his throat there fell

A voice from heaven upon him in his pride,

'Thy kingdom is departed:' and they drave

The madman from his palace: and he dwelt

With beasts and grazed their herbage, as the dews

Of heaven were wet upon him: till he knew

That the high God, to whom man's kings are dust,

Rules in the kingdom of the sons of men,

And delegates His power to whom He will.

This hast thou known, Belshazzar, yet refused

To humble thee before Him. Thou hast dared
To lift thyself against the Lord of heaven.
Thou hast defiled the vessels of His house
With idol wine, and given in these the praise
To gods of stone and silver; in whose mouth
There is no speech nor seeing in their eyes.
But the high God thou hast not glorified :
Is not thy breath as vapour in His hand,
And all thy ways as nothing in His sight?

Then came the hand of anger from the Lord,
And in thy feasting hour against the wall
It wrote; and word by word I will declare
The writing and assurance of thy doom.
MENE. Thy kingdom God hath numbered out
And finished it henceforward from the earth.
TEKEL. Thou in the balances art weighed,
And God hath found thee wanting utterly.
PERES. Thy kingdom is divided : God
Hath given it to the Persians and the Medes.

Nay, bring me no reward, no scarlet robe
Or chain of honour. Why should I desire
A barren title in a falling realm?
This and thy splendour are no longer thine.
The alien armies even now have scaled
Thy rampart, or have dried to their device
The mighty river's arm, and taught its wave
Another course. I forge no idle dream:
And even as I speak my words are deed.
Is there no sound upon the whispering night
Beyond this impious hall? Pale are ye now.
I hear the tread of armies: thou, O King,
Art nothing, for the Median will not spare.
Ye stand like sheep, and herd about the base
Of each dumb idol: surely these shall save,
For these are gods indeed, and they shall wake
From stony sleep and hurl the intruding host
Beyond Euphrates. They are gods indeed!
Down on thy knees, Belshazzar, for thy time

Is at its overthrow : thy sand is run :

Thy sceptre is departed evermore :

Entreat for mercy thine insulted God.

THE END.